Little Lisa And the
Neighborhood Block Party

Look for these and other books about Little Lisa in the Little Lisa Series:

#1 Little Lisa and the Neighborhood Block Party

#2 Little Lisa and the Go-Kart Chase

#3 Little Lisa and the Math Score

#4 Little Lisa Goes Crawfishing

Visit www.thesecretsistersclub.com

Little Lisa Series

Little Lisa And the Neighborhood Block Party

Dr. Alicia Holland

Illustrations by Khanh Bui

This book may be ordered through booksellers or by contacting:

iGlobal Educational Services, LLC
13785 Highway 183, Suite 125
Austin, Texas 78750
www.iglobaleducation.com
512-761-5898

Because of the dynamic nature of the Internet, any web addresses or links contained in this book may have changed since publication and may no longer be valid. The views expressed in this work are solely those of the author and do not necessarily reflect the views of the publisher, and the publisher hereby disclaims any responsibility for them.

This is a work of fiction. Names, characters, businesses, places, events, and incidents are either the products of the author's imagination or used in a fictitious manner. Any resemblance to actual persons, living or dead, or actual events is purely coincidental.

Little Lisa Series: Little Lisa and the Neighborhood Block Party

ISBN-13: 978-1-944346-14-0

Acknowledgements

I want to first honor God for placing in my heart to share my story with others. It was He whom brought Karen and I together to manifest this project. I am so grateful for Karen Hendry as she took my notes and helped write this fictitious book. There are truly no words to express my gratitude as you are truly a blessing.

I also want to thank Surendra Gupta for his creativity in formatting and Khanh Bui for his creativity in bringing life to the designs and illustrations in this book series. Both of you are amazing!

Dedication

I dedicate this book series to my beautiful and talented daughters, Georgia and Amaiya Johnson. Remember, you are valued, loved, and competent. You are worthy!

Chapter 1
The Block Party

I can hear Momma in the kitchen. The rattle of the pots and pans always tells me when Momma is making dinner. It's like a secret pot language that only I understand. I go into the kitchen and sit at the table. Momma wipes her hands on her blue flowered apron and then she starts to peel potatoes and put them in a big pot.

"Momma?" I say.

"Yes, sugar," says Momma, talking while she peels.

"Can we have a party?" I ask.

"A party?" Momma asks. "Whatever put that idea into your head?"

"Dancing."

"Dancing?" asks Momma, turning around from her supper preparations. "What does dancing have to do with having a party?"

"I wanna have a block party and invite all of my friends for a dance contest!" I say, bouncing up and down in the chair.

"Well, that sounds like a great idea, honey. Maybe your sister Michelle can help plan it."

"Will you help, too, Momma?"

"Of course I will, honey. But not right now cause I'm making dinner."

"OK." I get up from the table. "I'll go ask Michelle."

I look in Michelle's bedroom, but Michelle isn't in there. I go into the living room and look out the window. There is Michelle talking to a boy in the driveway. I run out the front door and yell, "Michelle!"

Michelle turns around and sees me and by the time I reach her, the boy is walking away down the street. "What is it, Lisa!" says Michelle. She sounds a little annoyed and kind of huffs when she talks.

"Sorry, Michelle," I say.

"It's okay," Michelle replies, putting her hand on my shoulder and walking back to their house with me. "What did you want?"

"Will you help me plan a block party so all my friends and I can have a dance contest?"

"Well, sure, squirt, but where are you gonna hold it?"

"I don't know," I say.

"Our house and yard aren't very big. Maybe Uncle Kenny would be willing, but you'll have to get Momma to ask."

"Okay, I will!" I run into the house to ask Momma.

After dinner, Momma and I walk to Uncle Kenny's house. He lives four blocks away, but on the same street, Lawrence Street, in Many, Louisiana. Many is a small city, but it's nice. I like living here, mostly because all my family is here. It's just where I belong.

When we go into Uncle Kenny's house, I am jumping up and down as Momma speaks. "Lisa wants to hold a block party and we were thinking your house would be a great spot."

I am nodding, "Yeah, your house is perfect. It's bigger than ours, with a bigger yard. Plus it's right in the middle of everywhere!"

"A block party, huh?" says Uncle Kenny. "You know Mal, Lisa, folks around here aren't used to parties." Momma's name is Mallori, but Uncle Kenny just calls her Mal.

"That's okay," I say. "They'll get used to it and they'll have fun because it's gonna be a dance party!"

"Well, when would this party happen?"

"I don't know," I say. I hadn't given it much thought. "This weekend?"

"That's too soon, honey," says Momma. "You need time to prepare."

"Next weekend?" I say.

"That would work better," says Momma. She turns to Uncle Kenny. "Well, Kenny, what do you think?"

Uncle Kenny stands there for forever, rubbing his chin with his hand, his brown eyes squinting slightly at me. Finally, he nods and I jump into the air with a whoop! Then I run and hug him and say, "Thank you!"

"Well, honey, you're welcome," says Uncle Kenny. "But now you gotta go home and plan all this out."

I nodd. "There is so much to do! I need to decide who to invite, put up posters, plan the food."

"Linelle Destiny Sycamores, you just hold on right there," says Momma. My real name is Linelle Destiny Sycamores, but my Gramma Lucy-Belle nicknamed me Little Lisa one time after we had a hurricane and that's what stuck. Everyone calls me that. "First, we need to go home and clean up from dinner. You have dishes to do."

"I know," I say. "But then I have a lot of work to do! This is gonna be awesome!"

"I know it will, honey," says Uncle Kenny, then he winks at Momma.

Momma and I say goodbye and I can't stop thinking about the block party the whole walk home. I feel like I could fly!

Chapter 2:
Planning the Party

The next morning, as soon as I open my eyes I pull out my notebook and look at what I wrote down yesterday evening. I made a list of the friends I want to invite:

- ♥ Brittany Townes
- ♥ Jennifer Davis
- ♥ Renee Pickles
- ♥ Mike Pryce
- ♥ Darren James

I love my friends, even though they are kind of crazy. I also wrote down some food ideas:

- ♥ Popcorn
- ♥ Hotdogs
- ♥ Freezies

OK, maybe I need some help in the food department. That's not much food and it's not exciting enough for my block party. If I want people to enjoy it, then I have to have exotic food.

Then there is the music to think of. Hmmm... What songs to use. After I had given it some thought, I wrote down a short list of songs:

♥ 'Whoomp! There It Is'
♥ 'The Chi-Chi Dance'
♥ 'Beat It'

I jump out of bed and get dressed. Brittany will be here soon because I called her last night and told her I had big news and she had to come over as soon as she woke up. She begged me to tell her over the phone, but I said, "No way!"

When I'm dressed, I go out on the front step and wait. And wait. And wait. Finally, when my tummy is starting to growl from hunger, Brittany shows up.

"Hi, Lisa," she says, "What's the big news?"

"Just a second," I say and I run into the house and grab a granola bar. When I'm back outside, I unwrap the granola bar and take a bite. Then I talk through a mouthful of granola bar. "I am planning a block party!"

"A block party?" asks Brittany.

"Yeah, a party for everyone. At my Uncle Kenny's house. It's going to be a dance party theme and we will have a dance contest and choose winners and everything! Plus, the people who aren't dancing in the contest will have great entertainment." I smile proudly and nod my head because of course I had thought of the most fantastic idea ever.

"That's a wonderful idea! Can I help?" asks Brittany. "Please?"

"Of course you can, silly. Why do you think I had you come over?" I get out my notebook, dropping my granola bar wrapper on the step beside me. "Here is what I have so far."

Brittany reads my lists, saying, "Mmmhmm…" and nodding her head as she traces down with her finger, purple nail polish glittering in the sunlight. "You should add the song 'What About Your Friends,'" says Brittany.

I take the notebook from her. "Good idea. I love that song," I say as I write the name of the song down.

"When are we having the block party?" asks Brittany.

"Next weekend."

"Awesome," says Brittany. "That gives us plenty of time to prepare."

"Michelle and Momma are going to help, too," I say.

"Okay, so what do you want me to do," asks Brittany.

"We need to start coming up with the dances for the songs. When we figure it out, we can teach everyone else."

"Sounds like a plan."

"But just wait because I need another granola bar." I dash in and grab another granola bar so I can fuel up. I have a busy day ahead of me.

Chapter 3:
Dance Moves

It's been two days since I decided to hold a block party and preparations are well underway. Momma has been helping when she has spare time, which isn't much because she works two jobs. But it's Saturday and she has the afternoon off.

She is humming a tune, I don't know what it is, and is working on organizing a stage for us to perform on. Momma just loves planning things and she is very good at it. My birthday parties are always the best out of all my friends and I know Momma wants our block party to be perfect.

Michelle is taking care of the food for the party. Since I need something better than hot dogs and freezies, Michelle said she would make sure we have something yummy to eat. She comes into the house with some bags from the grocery store and me and my friends, Brittany, Renee, Darren, and Mike, follow her to the kitchen.

"What did you get?" I ask Michelle as she sets the bags on the table.

"Chill out, squirt," Michelle says as she brushes something off her white tank top and then begins pulling things out of the bag. I see her pull out popcorn and apples and sugar and cream. I don't get what they are for and I look at my friends and shrug my shoulders.

Michelle must see me because she says, "These are just the ingredients. I'm going to make candy apples and popcorn balls. They will be easy for people to hold onto and eat while watching the dance contest."

"Mmmmmm...," we all say together.

Then I say, "Michelle, would you help us with some dance moves? We aren't sure what to do."

"Sure. Just let me put these groceries away and I'll meet you out front."

We are on the front lawn practicing the moves we know when Michelle comes out of the house. We are moving our feet back and forth and clapping our hands, the ghetto blaster blaring "What About Your Friends."

"Well, now I see why you need my help," jokes Michelle.

But we all nod because we really do need her help.

"Okay, you all line up here and I'll show you a few moves. Then you can takes those and choreograph a dance with them."

"Choreograph?" says Darren.

"Make up moves for the dance that go with the music."

Darren nods and gets into line beside me.

"First, you need to know how to spin." Michelle demonstrates an awesome spin, which looks so cool in her tank top and mini skirt. She glows in the sun as she spins. "Now you try," she says.

We all spin and Renee keeps spinning until she falls down. I help her up.

"That wasn't bad," says Michelle, "but the idea is to stay on your feet. You want to look graceful and balanced."

They tried the spin again.

"Better," says Michelle. "Now, do this." She spins again with her arms held close to her, but at the end of the spin she jumps out so her legs are held wide and her arms are in the air.

We copy the move and she nods her approval. "Now this one is a little trickier. You need to shake your hips like this." She puts her hands on her hips and shakes them just like we've seen dancers do in music videos.

We all try it. I think it's harder than it looks. We collapse on the ground in a fit of giggles. Michelle is standing there with her hands still on her hips, staring at us with a smile on her face.

"Okay, guys come on," I say.

We all get up and Michelle shows us again. We practice a few times until Michelle finally says, "I think you guys have it, but there is one more thing you absolutely have to do when you are performing and it's more important than any of these moves."

"What's that?" I say.

"You have to smile. Big smiles, too, which is hard when you're concentrating on getting the moves right. So practice smiling while you're dancing. That way the people who are watching you will know you're having fun. Plus, when you smile, it makes the dance look easier than it is." Michelle ends off with a few dance moves, smiling the whole time.

"Wow, thanks, Michelle," says Brittany.

"Anytime. Now you guys work out a dance using those moves. Keep smiling and practice."

Michelle goes into the house and we get to it. We have a lot of work to do.

Chapter 4:
Disagreement

On Sunday, just after lunch, someone knocks on my front door. I run from the kitchen to answer the door, still licking the peanut butter off of the roof of my mouth because there was too much on my sandwich, and my cousin Jennifer is standing at the door.

"I heard you're having a dance party," Jennifer exhales, as if she had been waiting, holding it all in until someone opened the door.

"Hi Jenn," I say. "Yes, we are. Do you want to do it with us?"

"Oh yes, please!" Jennifer shouts as she jumps up and down, her curly hair bouncing along with her. "I absolutely love dancing!"

"Awesome, Jenn. We started putting the dance together yesterday and it's pretty much worked out, but you can learn it easy. They'll all be here soon to practice."

"Yay! Plus, I can help with the choreography, if you need any. I am on the pep squad, after all."

Jennifer came inside and we went to find Michelle. The others hadn't arrived yet, so Michelle went into the backyard with me and Jennifer and taught Jennifer the dance we had made up.

Just when Jennifer is getting the hang of the dance, Renee shows up. Five minutes later, Mike and Darren appear. Brittany is last, which is surprising because she is usually the first one there.

"Sorry," says Brittany. "I was just about to leave when my mom gave me some chores to do. I did them as fast as I could." She notices Jennifer and says, "Hi, Jenn. You joining us?"

"I sure am!" says Jennifer.

The group spends about a half an hour practicing the dance and Jennifer suggests a couple of additions to the choreography that everyone likes.

Then Mike says, "Everyone needs to know about this block party! It's going to be so awesome!"

"Why don't you go tell everyone about it, then," says Darren.

"I think I will," says Mike. "Wanna come with me, Lisa?"

"No thanks," I say. "I'll stay here and work on the dance some more."

"Suit yourself." Mike runs off and we can hear him shouting out loud telling everyone to come to the block party next weekend.

"That is one crazy dude," says Darren.

Then Jennifer pipes up and says, "What about solos?"

"Solos?" I say.

"Yeah, people taking turns dancing by themselves. I wouldn't mind doing a dance on my own."

I think about the idea of solos. Mike's voice is faint in the background, but I can still hear it. "I was kind of hoping this would be a group effort," I say.

"I think dancing a solo would be fun," says Renee.

"I could dig that," says Darren.

"But won't it be hard to dance together as a group and then split up and do solos?" I say.

"Not at all," says Jennifer. "We can just add parts in. That way, everyone who wants to will get a chance to shine on their own in front of our audience."

I can feel the frown on my face. Brittany joins in the conversation and says, "I think we should shine as a group. That's what we have practiced for and that was the idea from the beginning."

"I just think the dance could be better if we had some solos," says Jennifer. Renee and Darren nod their agreement.

Mike comes running into the backyard and stops short. He can see the looks on everyone's faces. "What's going on guys?"

"Some of us would like to perform solos in the dance, but Lisa says no," snaps Jennifer.

Just then Michelle walks up to them. "I've heard enough of this argument to know what's going on," she says. "Listen, guys, let's chill. I get what you're saying, but we started this as a team and we should finish it as a team. There is no reason why you can all so the dance together as planned."

"Well," says Jennifer, "I want to do my own thing, too. That would make it more fun."

Darren nods his head. "Some step dancing would go down real well," he says. "Being out there by myself, jammin' it in front of the crowd. Sweet!"

Mike hadn't said a word since he got back, but he speaks up and says, "Look, I think we should all stick with the plan. After all, this was Lisa's idea."

"That doesn't mean she's the boss," says Renee.

I look at Michelle, the worry plain on my face. She shrugs her shoulders at me. We are stumped.

"I have to go now," Jennifer says, although I'm sure she could stay longer if she wanted to.

"Yeah, me, too," says Renee. "Bye Lisa. Bye everyone."

The two girls leave and everyone else says their goodbyes and soon the backyard is empty except me and Michelle.

I turn to Michelle, fighting back the tears. "What are we gonna do?"

"Don't worry, squirt. I know this feels bad, but everything is gonna work out just fine. I promise."

I nod and we go inside to plan other parts of the block party. I hope Michelle is right.

Chapter 5:
Party Day!

My eyes pop open and I jump out of bed immediately. It doesn't take me any time to wake up this morning. I set my clothes out last night so I would be ready to go today. I don't want to be late. I picked out a brightly colored tank top with a cool design on it and a matching green skirt for the big day. I want to look nice.

I run into the kitchen and Momma is there, frying up pancakes. "I thought you could use a good breakfast before you head out to get the party started."

"Thanks, Momma," I say, giving her a big hug. I sit down at the table and she puts a plate of pancakes in front of me. I pour on the syrup and start eating.

"Slow down, child. You gonna choke to death on some of that food."

"Sorry, Momma." I slow down, a little.

When I'm done I take my plate to the sink and kiss Momma on the cheek. Then I race out the front door and down the street to help get everything ready at Uncle Kenny's house.

It's 1:00, when the party is scheduled to begin, and I can't believe how many people there are! I've never seen so many people in one place, except at our assemblies at school, but there are always lots of kids at a school. This is different. There are so many adults and people of all ages. It's the first block party we have ever had in our neighborhood. People must really like parties!

I am bouncing up and down with excitement. So are all my friends. "This is so amazing!" says Brittany. I nod my head in agreement. There are still people arriving by quarter past one and I look up at Momma and Uncle Kenny. Momma takes my hand and squeezes it and Uncle Kenny winks at me, a big smile on his face. I can see Michelle over at the refreshment table, making sure all the food and drinks are ready.

Darren is hosting the party. He does all the announcements and talking. Momma told me he is called the Master of Ceremonies or MC for short. I think Darren is perfect for the job. He loves talking. At school his teacher has a hard time getting Darren to stop talking.

Darren gets up on a special platform Uncle Kenny had in his garage. The he shouts out to everyone. "Hello and welcome to the Lawrence Street block party!"

Some of the crowd closest to Darren quiets down to hear him and he shouts it out again. Soon, everyone is quiet and waiting to hear what Darren has to say.

Darren shouts out to be sure everyone hears him. "This afternoon is going to be crazy fun!" Everyone cheers. When they are quiet again Darren says, "I'm going to give you the lay of the land. First, we will have music playing throughout the afternoon, thanks to Mr. Kenny Sweets, who has let us hold this party at his house." Everyone cheers and Uncle Kenny waves a hand.

Darren is beaming, his blue muscle shirt rippling in the light breeze. He continues, "The lovely Michelle Sycamores has made some great food for y'all. She has popcorn balls, candied apples, and lemonade to quench your thirst. You can find her and all the goodies at the table over there." He points to his left.

"And the dance contest will be held over there," Darren points to his right. "We will begin the dances at 2:00, so anyone who wants to sign up can come and do that with me as soon as I am done up here." More cheering. "We also need three volunteers to be judges for the contest. You can sign up with me if you would like to do this. Finally, for the younger kids, we have an area set up in Mr. Sweets' driveway where they can draw with chalk and jump rope."

I can see there are already kids over there, drawing big flowers and things. One boy even drew a rocket ship.

"I guess that's it," says Darren. "Except that y'all should just have fun!"

Everyone lets out a huge cheer and Darren jumps down to talk to anyone who wants to sign up for the dance contest. There is a long line forming and he starts writing down the names. He is so good at being an MC. Maybe he can get a job doing it somewhere. Anyone would hire him! But right now me and my friends have to get ready for our dance. I just hope it won't be a problem because we still haven't settled our argument about the solos.

Chapter 6:
Friction

I have to get everyone together and talk about our dance. I know that some of my friends still want to do solos and we don't have much time to figure this out. It's 1:30 and the dance contest starts in half an hour!

It seems as though my friends are thinking the same thing as me because they are gathering together nearby. I walk over and they are already at it, arguing about doing solos and dancing on their own.

Jenn is speaking as I walk up to the group. "I know exactly what I want to do for my solo. My moves are great." She spins and does a fancy move none of us have even learned.

I can see Brittany's eyes glance my way and the look on her face tells the others I'm coming. They all go quiet and I feel like turning around and walking away. But I don't. I look each one of them in the eye and I look at Jenn last. "We are a team," I say. "We need to start acting like one."

"Well, it feels as though we're *your* team and we have to do what you say," says Renee.

"That's not true!" I say. "Most of the dance moves were made up by other people. I haven't even really done all that much when it comes to our dance choreography."

Jenn pipes up. "Exactly! So why do you get to decide that we can't do solos? I don't think that's fair."

"Because we are supposed to be dancing together. That's the way we planned it, to enter the contest as a team."

I can see Michelle looking over at us from the food table. Her friend Carlette is with her and Michelle says something to Carlette and then starts walking toward us, her high heels clicking on the pavement. As she walks up to the group she looks at me and I shake my head.

"Are we still having the same argument about solos?" Michelle asks the group.

Everyone nods. Darren comes up to us and says, "Everyone is signed up and there's just 20 minutes to go, guys. We should run through our dance again before it starts."

"We would if we knew what we were doing," says Jenn. "Lisa still doesn't approve of solos." The tone of her voice is so mean and I struggle not to lose it and cry in front of them.

Michelle says, "You know guys, it's really important to finish what you start and it's important to think of others, not just yourselves. You began this dance together and it doesn't seem fair to change the rules half way through."

"Lisa isn't thinking of others. She just wants the dance her way," says Renee.

"That's not true!" I shout. "I want the dance to be a little bit of all of us. We worked so hard to create a dance we all like and I don't see any reason to change it. It's awesome the way it is. It's *ours* the way it is."

Brittany and Mike nod. Darren looks like he wants to be anywhere else but there. Renee and Jenn are standing with their arms crossed, like they just aren't prepared to budge. I can hear the crowd of people all around us, laughing and having fun. People are walking around with candy apples and cups of lemonade. But here we are, standing around getting mad at each other, while everyone else has fun. Maybe our dance won't work out after all. It definitely won't if we can't work together.

Michelle has a thoughtful look on her face and then she turns around and walks away. But she isn't going back to the food table. She is heading into Uncle Kenny's house. I hope she comes back soon because I don't know what to do and we don't have much time.

Chapter 7:
Truth

It hasn't been long since Michelle left, but I can see her coming back and she isn't alone. She has Momma with her and I know what she is doing. If anyone can sort out this mess, it's Momma. And it's a good thing, too, because the dance contest starts in 15 minutes!

I leave the group and walk over to meet Michelle and Momma. "Here ya go, squirt. Momma to the rescue." With that, Michelle ruffles my hair and whispers, "Everything will work out fine." Then she heads back to the food table.

Momma looks at me and then says, "Lead the way, child. I'll see what I can do to help."

I nod and we walk back over to my friends. It doesn't take them long to realize Momma is with me and they all say, "Hi, Mrs. Sycamores."

"Hi," Momma responds. "Now, I hear y'all havin' a problem agreeing on your dance."

Everyone nods.

"I also hear that y'all made an agreement at the beginnin' to work as a team and do a dance together."

Everyone nods again.

"So what is all this nonsense about changing things up after you have made a dance and agreed on it?"

No one answers at first, but then Jenn speaks up. "Well, Auntie Mallori. Some of us decided we really want to do solo dances."

"Was this something you kids talked about doing in the beginning?"

Everyone shakes their head.

"Had you already designed a dance that you all liked?" asks Momma.

Everyone nods their head.

"Well, it seems to me," says Momma, "that you shouldn't go changing up something that everyone agreed on unless everyone agrees with the changes."

Jenn is about to open her mouth to say something, but Momma puts up her hand to silence her. "Now, just a minute. I want you to know that it's better to work as a team. Do y'all know why?"

"No," some of us say, while others shake their head. But Brittany speaks up and says, "Because it's more fun."

"Child, you are right!" says Momma. "But it's more than that. When you work as a team, you have friends and other people who watch out for you. But if y'all are by yourself, then you are all alone."

Momma watches everyone as they think about what she is saying. Darren says, "Excuse me, Mrs. Sycamores. I have to go make an announcement that the dance contest starts in 10 minutes."

Momma nods and Darren runs off. A moment later, we hear him calling out, "Attention everyone! There is only 10 minutes left before the dance contest starts. Would those who signed up for the contest please begin making their way to line up here." Darren indicates his left, which is along the edge of Uncle Kenny's front yard.

People start walking past us, heading over to where the dance performances will be. Momma continues, "Being a team is important. When y'all are part of a team, you have someone to help you up when you fall. If you're by yourself, you have no one to dance with."

Again, Momma pauses to let her words sink in.

"Best of all," Momma continues, "If y'all are part of a team, you can all be winners by encouraging and congratulating one another. If you're on your own, you don't have anyone to hug, but if you are a team, then you can share your joy with each other and have a group hug!"

Some of my friends are nodding. Even Renee's head is moving up and down ever so slightly. Momma looks at me and winks. Then she speaks to the group. "Now, I know y'all will make the right decision because y'all are smart kids. Just think about what's really important."

Momma walks away, heading over to get a good spot to watch the dances. I watch her go, then look back at my friends. What next, I wonder. Darren comes back and looks at everyone. Then his eyes settle on me and I shrug. I wait to see what my friends will do.

Chapter 8:
Thinking Hard

Me and my friends just stand there looking at each other after Momma leaves and for a few moments no one says a word. Then Darren breaks the silence. "I have to go announce the dance contest starts in five minutes, but I think I'm with Lisa on this. No point in breaking up the team, especially this close to the contest."

Darren runs off, leaving the rest of us standing there to figure this out. We can hear his voice shouting, "Five minutes until the ultimate dance contest begins!"

"Well," I say, "whatever we decide to do, we had better decide now. We don't have much time left."

Brittany nods. "I'm with you, Lisa."

"You always were with Lisa," says Jenn. "No change there."

"Yeah and I always was with Lisa because I would rather go into this together, the way we planned, and have fun with my friends than go into it with all of us being angry with each other. There is no fun in any of this if we are all mad."

Renee finally speaks up. "Mrs. Sycamores made some good points. I mean, isn't the point of all this to have fun together and support each other as a team? Plus, I know I would feel a lot more foolish if I messed up by myself than if I messed up with a team behind me."

We all nod, except Jenn, whose face is all scrunched up like she is thinking really hard.

"Come on, Jenn," I say. "I want all of us to be together. We all want all of us to be together." Everyone nods again and waits for Jenn to say something.

"I guess it would be nice to shine together and help each other out. And it would be way more embarrassing to make a mistake when you're up there by yourself. Maybe being all alone up there isn't as fun after all, especially if we're all mad at each other."

"Yay!" shouts Brittany. We all jump up and down.

Then we hear Darren announce, "Attention everyone. The dance contest starts in two minutes. Would everyone who signed up please come and line up here so I can put you in the order you singed up in?"

I look at Jenn. "Well?" I say.

Jenn sighs. "Okay, I'm in. If this is what everyone is happy with, I'll do it the way it was originally planned. I guess it'll still be fun."

"Of course it'll be fun!" I say and I give Jenn a hug.

Everyone shouts and cheers and slaps Jenn on the back, thanking her for making the decision to stick with the team.

"We have to go over and tell Darren," I say. "He needs to add our names to the list."

We all run over and Darren can tell just by the looks on our faces that we are doing it. He starts adding our names to the list before we even reach him. "We're on!" I say when we stop next to him.

"That's awesome, guys," he says. "And since we are at the end of the list, we are going to be the grand finale!"

Everyone likes the sound of that. We go to the end of the lineup of contestants and wait. The lineup is long and I am so happy so many people are participating. There are even a couple of adults in the lineup.

Then Brittany says, "Oh, wait. I have something for everyone." She reaches into her bag and pulls out some white gloves. "For when we dance to 'Beat It.'"

"This is awesome," says Jenn, putting the glove on her right hand. "Thanks!"

Everyone loves the gloves and we wait for the contest to begin. What a perfect day!

Chapter 9:
Dance Fever!

Finally, it's time. Darren steps onto the "stage," which is just the middle of Uncle Kenny's front lawn and announces the first dancers, Chloe Purplefoot, Katriya Tyler, and Darla Stineberry. They will be dancing to Rhythm Is A Dancer. Three middle school girls give Darren their music and get ready to dance. I recognize them, but I don't know them that well.

Everyone who is dancing has their music with them already or had time to go home and get it so that Darren can play it for them. Darren puts the first CD in and starts the song and the girls begin their dance. They look pretty good and they obviously had time to practice.

I look around and see all the people watching the dancing. Some people brought lawn chairs to sit on. Little kids are wiggling and dancing along while they stand next to their parents. Others are running around their parents' legs or chairs, chasing each other. Everyone is enjoying the music, clapping along and watching the dancing.

When the first group is done, Darren continues to announce the dancers as their turn comes up and play the music for them. Everyone is thrilled with the dances and I see so many of the adults talking about the good dancing and the talent of all the dancers.

Brittany nudges me with her elbow. "Some of these dances are really good," she whispers.

I nod. "I know. Especially the first group of dancers."

"Are you nervous?" asks Brittany.

"A little," I reply.

"Me, too."

There are so many dancers it takes a long time to go through them all. But the weather is nice, it's warm and the sun is shining. Everyone is enjoying themselves.

Then the dancers lined up right in front of my group are up. That means we're next. A chill runs through my body and I feel so excited. I watch their dance, but really I'm thinking about ours. We were so busy arguing about the solos and everything that we didn't get a chance to practice it before the contest started. I just hope everyone remembers what to do.

Then Darren announces our group. He asks someone in the audience to press play on the ghetto blaster when he gives a signal and then he joins us. We get ourselves set and Darren nods. We put on our white Michael Jackson gloves and the music starts. We go through the dance flawlessly. We spin around when we were supposed to, shake our hips just like Michelle taught us to, and do the moves Jenn taught us. Everything flows together to make a perfect dance.

When the dance is over, everyone cheers. Darren waits until it gets quiet and then he thanks everyone, all the dancers and the people who watched. Everyone cheers again and we all give each other high fives. Then I run over to Momma and give her a big hug.

"Well, now sugar," Momma says. "What's all this for?"

"Thank you for helping my friends decide to dance together," I say.

"Well, you're welcome, child, but you know, they already knew all what I told 'em. They just needed remindin', that's all."

I nod. Then Momma says, "You know, people were telling me how talented y'all are. You did good."

"Thanks, Momma." Then I run off to be with my friends. We go over to the food table, but there isn't anything left, just some lemonade. We are disappointed, but then Carlette grabs a box from under the table and inside is a popcorn ball and candy apple for each of us.

"Michelle's got y'all covered," says Carlette.

We all dig in and enjoy the food. I have to remember to thank Michelle later. We eat and wait for the judging to begin.

Chapter 10:
Winners

I'm sipping my lemonade and waiting with my friends for the judges to announce the winners. It's been a few minutes since the dance contest ended and people have been chatting and having fun while the three judges talk to each other. One of the judges, Mrs. Mavis Brown, lives four houses down from me. The other two, Mrs. Judy Duckworth and Mr. Clay Denim, I don't know very well, but Momma and Pop know them. When it comes down to it, I suppose everyone knows everyone else. Many, Louisiana is a small town.

Finally, Mrs. Brown walks onto the dance area. "Hello, everyone!" It takes time for everyone to realize the judges are ready and to quiet down. I can hear people shushing those around them. The sound of people saying "Shhh" spreads through the crowd, from the front to the back, like a wave.

Once everyone is quiet, Mrs. Brown speaks. "We had such a hard time choosin' winners for this dance contest. Y'all were so good. I was a real nice time for us all." Everyone cheers.

"We really didn't want to pick anyone specific as winners because we really felt you were all winners. But since we had the job of choosing the best dances, we narrowed it down to the top three." More cheers from the crowd.

Mrs. Brown continues, "I will announce the third-place winners first, followed by second place and first place." She looks down at the paper she is holding. "Our third place winners are Jessie Minnow and Dina Gemstone! They were wonderful!"

Everyone cheers loudly and claps for the duo. They are second-graders at my school.

"Come on up, now," says Mrs. Brown and Jessie and Dina walk up to stand next to Mrs. Brown.

"Our second-place winners are Little Lisa Sycamores, Renee Pickles, Brittany Townes, Jennifer Davis, Mike Pryce, and Darren James!" I'm stunned. There were so many great dances. I didn't think we would be one of the best.

We all look at each other and then we jump up and down, shouting a chorus of "Yes!" Then we all run over to stand beside Mrs. Brown.

"Congratulations," she says to us. "And now, I would like to announce the first-place winners of today's dance contest."

This is so exciting. I can't wait to find out who the winner is. I can hear Darren doing a drumroll behind me. Other people join in. Then Mrs. Brown says, "Please give a big round of applause to the first dance act we saw today, performed by Chloe Purplefoot, Katriya Tyler, and Darla Stineberry!"

The crowd erupts with cheering as the three girls come forward. They have huge smiles on their faces and they look totally surprised. When they reach us and stand beside us, we all begin to congratulate each other. Everyone is so supportive.

"I thought for sure you guys would win," Katriya says to me. "Your dance was amazing."

"Thanks," I say. "You guys were amazing, too. You deserved to win."

Mrs. Brown says, "Thank you, everyone, for joining use today! And thank you to the Sycamores family for organizing such a terrific block party!"

At that, everyone cheers louder than ever before. The next thing I know, my friends have lifted me up high on their shoulders to carry me around. I feel better than I ever have in my whole life!

After the cheering dies down and my friends put me down, we all stand looking at each other. Then Jenn speaks up. "That was really fun, guys. I know I wanted to do a solo and break up the team, but honestly, if I had won, it wouldn't have been nearly as fun without a team to share it with."

"Definitely," says Renee.

Everyone else nods.

"I'm so glad we worked it out," I say. "And I'm glad you all did this with me. You're all such great friends."

As we are hugging each other, Michelle comes over. "I'm so happy you guys worked it out," she says.

"Thanks, Michelle," says Brittany.

"And thanks for saving us some of the food," I say. "It was delicious!"

"No problem, squirt."

"Excuse me," I say and then I run over to where Uncle Kenny is standing. "Uncle Kenny?"

"Yes, my Little Lisa."

"I just wanted to thank you for letting us have this block party at your house."

"You are most welcome, darlin'," says Uncle Kenny, giving me a hug. "You did a good job. I'm proud of you."

"Thanks," I say. I realize that I'm actually pretty proud of myself. I did a lot of work, but I had a lot of help, too. I feel really good as we clean up and get ready to go home. I wonder what's in store for me next.

About the Author

Alicia Linelle Holland was born and raised in Many, Louisiana and got her middle name after her mother, Vera Linelle. When Alicia was in middle school, she started the Secret Sister Club that you read about in the Linelle Destiny Book Series. Alicia Holland has been working towards bringing back the Secret Sister Club as she embarks upon quite an interesting life and spiritual journey. At age 26, she earned her Doctorate in Education so that she can be in a position to help others believe in themselves and go far. At age 31, Dr. Alicia Holland opened a Not for Profit, Alise Spiritual Healing & Wellness Center and was officially ordained as a Minister. As a Transformational Life Coach, Professor, Author, Speaker, and Minister, Dr. Holland travels the World sharing her message: "You are Loved, You are Valued, and You are Competent.

Dr. Alicia Holland has two beautiful daughters, ages 7 and 9, who travels the World with her and are active participants in the Secret Sister Club Mentoring Program. She and her family resides in Austin, Texas and are currently looking for a new puppy.

Dr. Holland is available for speaking engagements and can be reached at support@thesecretsistersclub.com or support@iglobaleducation.com.